ARCHIPE

G000095616

She is a swimmer bursting out of the sm̶ recent American years, out into a ris̶ beyond the poem-as-commodity into so̶r̶ ̶ ̶g̶ ̶ ̶a̶t̶e̶r̶, a continuity of articulate presence. There's something Wagnerian about Siegel's work, a sense of 'endless melody' undistracted by conventions of closure and easy formal strategies. It's brave, because it doesn't give the reader easy units to grasp. Instead, her poetry strives into openness, lives up to the deepest challenge of the past century, creating not artifacts but processes, long dances for agile readers.

Robert Kelly

Resonant and stylized, *Archipelago* is full of big questions about how to best live, how to speak and what to say, how to have empathy, in short, how to be and be attentive to the complications of this time, a time that might just be an apocalypse, but an apocalypse that is probably the beginning not the ending. Poetry has a long and esteemed tradition of inquiry, of philosophizing. *Archipelago* meets this tradition and raises it, asks it question after question.

Juliana Spahr

The speed of thought—not some rapid pulse or lickety-split rhythmicity (Alana Siegel's pulse is even enough); but as I let fit the movement of my reading to the movement of her language, I sense a lightning velocity to the flash of her intelligence; the work of relation and resonance that is operative behind the screen of speech; the work of mind and heart that allows for rich and multi-phasic connections wrought in image, sound, reference, and soul's release, to find their proper interval without requiring pause or interrupt to wrest encrypted sense from surface seas of text so that I am ever with her, far far out on the farthest reach of her *Archipelago*.

Charles Stein

ARCHIPELAGO

Alana Siegel

Station Hill
of Barrytown

© 2014 Alana Siegel

Published by Station Hill Press, Inc., 120 Station Hill Road, Barrytown, NY 12507, as a project of the Institute for Publishing Arts, Inc., in Barrytown, New York, a not-for-profit, tax-exempt organization [501 (c) (3)].

 This publication is supported in part by grants from the New York State Council on the Arts, a state agency.

Online catalog: www.stationhill.org
E-mail: publishers@stationhill.org

Interior design by Alana Siegel
Cover design by Susan Quasha with Alana Siegel

Library of Congress Cataloging-in-Publication Data
Siegel, Alana.
Archipelago / by Alana Siegel.
     pages cm
ISBN 978-1-58177-132-9
I. Title.
PS3619.I373A73 2013
813'.6—dc23
                              2013010136

Manufactured in the United States of America

Visita Interiora Terrae Rectificando Invenies Occultum Lapidem

for Robert

Contents

COMMUNION
(a preludium)

Communion

I do not want to be romanced. I want to be known as water in a glass is seen, taken in. A stranger is sheltered. The stranger is honored, by the blue and black tribe in the desert.

Hearts of wandering men walking in the burning sand become each other. They long for each other as they wander.

A parakeet strings its feathers across a laundry line, leaving to dry what covered its fragile bird heart.

The language it doesn't know, it leaves for the sun to landscape—it lays out, to anyone or anything that may see, glimpse, the yearning of its feathers to feel.

He said, "The Dharma cannot be known but it can be experienced."

A chord is struck, momentarily, a note is played. A color overtakes the signal of the bird—cellular—a color, a cell, a promise for how it coats what was once a call.

"If you know how to supplicate, do so."

He said when he was young, traveling in a foreign country, he saw people wasting away with flies on their faces. He wanted to brush the flies away, say to them in simple words,

"You can live. I promise I will not heave the word *heaven* upon you, or any word like it. But I can tell you there are worlds different from the world you live in. I know, I have come from one."

Bound to the seemingly inescapable, they were letting life trespass permission.

At a point you must return to arguing with the angels, demanding
new angles to rearrange your self-created eidolon of who you are to
be and are—

Highest image of my heart break forth from me!
Momentarily reveal how I am to see you or any other form

Me is a word we gave to our pain
For the life that longs to hear between two shells
Just this passing, this sorrow I see scale up the side of the building

He bound his heart to the front of his brain
This is what the box is for—a prayer is what our third eye asks for
Hides
The shout with no meaning except
Hearken

V'ahavta
Love me with all your heart, with all your might
With everything you have

Not because I want
Or need anything from you
I want you to feel I am everything you are

Matchbox you can't find, number you haven't called yet
Thought about your next thought

And one day awaken
Alone in the forest
This he says
Is the silence I meant
It has no meaning
It is not silent

What do you think from one moment to the next?
How do you know the name of what is in front of you?

Someone must have told me once—this is called a fork, and this—a
knife. Or maybe after so many restaurants, hearing the names said, I
came to know the names. Or maybe I knew the names not by hearing
them. I knew them before I grew into them. Maybe I knew the names
before I knew my life, these vestiges of language. Maybe the names
know me more than me, are great vessels I am granted to enter only
when I say them.

My prayer is not asking the world to be any way. My prayer is not
asking to be given a thing. You asked me, "What can I do for you?"
But you are one whose gift to me is giving me nothing, sitting inside,
opening the doors of your mind. A door flings open to an Italian
villa, rolling green Tuscan hills. An old eye is the key. Sorrow is the
door.

Watch as the lips taste one more time—animal pull that makes me
feel medieval, causes me to resort to drastic measures, abstain from
the sweetness that is life's tip.

What I mean feels only wrong because it is more, less than, beyond
being ensconced in the subjects of your thinking, your baseline
dramas that scourge divinity, plague sense with boring please.

I sue the random, echo gravity, twist for existence a new name.

My life is my words, are my names, they are yours
Her skirt is not a grass skirt
It is a skirt of sky

She left but left the sky with me
A piece of cloth I make my word

Every word I speak is a word flesh needs
Life taking life from life

Are you ready to read The Book of Life?

Ready means read
The adverb of books
The moments that have passed us by

Books make stronger moments
Demand a deeper bond with time

Do not rise up to me, fly away as the little wisps of dandelion

I admire the flowers but I am not a flower
I am an old woman who wants to be older than words

Older than time
Older than what stone invokes

Youth arrests me, photographs my fingers
Roots receiving sounds from an inhuman center

Core, I care
Ache of sky
My face a beach

Cloud words fall and say I love you

ARCHIPELAGO

How Do I Speak With Or Hold Or Return Or Cherish Or Understand

This deluge we casually call yesterday tomorrow and today?

In the hope of a swirling, paramount of tongues
Breaching inconsequence with exotic care

Seashelled inside incessant wars of men of mind
He lets rain settle on his fingertips

If all the universe is language
Or, if
The universe is only language

What we are is land in water
Or water is alone
Land is all we have

Island to find
Ocean, water of all we have but never find
Lost at sea or lost in land

Language me as chain

The History Of Language Is Not The History Of The World Soul

My grandfather and grandmother are standing next to each other—
young and cheerful, inside a field of light laughter, each wearing
black-framed glasses. My grandmother walks over to my grandfather,
holding a photograph of herself next to her grandmother.

As she approaches my grandfather, she turns the photograph over.
On the back is written an 87—she laughs to herself, crosses it out,
replaces the 87 with an 88. There is writing in German she reads out
loud—

> "The History of Language Is Not The History Of The
> World Soul. Rather, as Meister Eckhart says,

> > 'The History of Language is the words spoken
> > from father to daughter, father to son,
> > sister to brother—
> > and these words are equivalent
> > to the vast collection
> > of all the lines
> > of independent esoteric teachings.' "

The light in the eyes is given a name
Geared into a magnetic rhetoric

A matrix of world
Where what we call
Civilization, History, Culture, Tradition

Comes to feed and thrives
On the light in our eyes

Suddenly we have been speaking—

These words must be what they call angels, innocents
Friendships of the unjustified and the unjustifiable
Wings, from which we later taper thinking

Apocalypse. Is not the world always ending, not always beginning?

Has not the earth already ended, always?
Have we not died enough to not fear death anymore in life?

Any fear of death must mean you are not dead enough
Apocalypse as a great death
A failure in reverence to what is not time

If you think all of this will end at a point in time
Do you claim to live in any living understanding
Of what the word timeless stands for?

Timeless meaning what is not time
A being completely not any part of this
If what we are is what we cannot imagine we are—

Or Apocalypse
In its irreverence
Is backwardsly in service
Of the ritual sacrifice still speaking itself through
The animal we name time

Imagining killing
All we know to be ourselves
Fantasizing a cataclysmic ending
Because we cannot do it every day

See ourselves, not ourselves, nothing to be ourselves
Not even the Earth itself

Momentarily What We Are, Fighting What We Are

I wonder when he speaks to me if his voice becomes
The voice I could call my own, so the mind

Will loosen to what the heart wants to say
Straight from the pink rose no one is to see

Why is something I have seen prior to seeing now so dear to me?

Echo, Memory

The heart shaped bowl I took out from the cupboard

Next to the sink in the house I grew up in
Was my own heart, and this was my memory

And this was the heartbreak and the beauty of memory
That where you have been is where your heart lives

And memory will lead you to your heart

We Only Remember Poetry

A book in the ear
Can be remembered in the air

In this atmosphere
Strictly amnesiac

A way of positioning
Ugly earth in the oasis
Of its fact of being

And by this they are beautiful

Who was I then when I

To find within this know-
Ledge of finding oneself inside

What repeats if you do not find
Yourself inside

The mollusk
Pink seashell of gathering storm
Illustrate breath

Lizardly blue ascends
Waterfall slivers

Embrace within the business
Of being believed

To bustle towards her
The earth learns

How she castles to occur
Trusted, a worker of the earth

Time sees reflections of
Impossible desires
A jungle of balloons in which I am a child

A bird died in front of me
A tree fell before I saw it fall

To a God of Language

Your bird eye flashes
Between my upper lip
And my nose

Let me come to language
I have come
To the body
I have been silent
In feeling
Walking down roads

Samsara sleeps in anger dwelling swerving human violin weakening
Visions visit volts
Clarity cavity
Watching volition

How is wisdom not everything but a word
How is wisdom not
How is wisdom not everything utterly but a word
How is wisdom not utterly a word
How is a word not utterly everything
How is a word not a word

How Long Will It Take To Undo Time

I kissed him with my eyes closed, my lips tracing the clock
Melting into overture

If this means being here
Let my eyes be opened, raised

To the sores of common pentacles
To the hurt light on metallic bars craving shadow

A purple flower hovers above disfigured rock

> Information does not exist, or is, when you
> Are of-the-formation

> Arm-in-arm
> No less than, no better than

> What you were of the mind to
> Re-search and de-scribe

"The internet is not beautiful," I shouted
She moaned, "Why have we never asked ourselves this question?"

Breath, not only air
A secret of fire in no need of anything found

Undresses light into glamorous contours of origins
Grammars, from which

Animals seek shelter, beg
For the records of their ancient happiness
Hidden away in tombs of sense

There Is A Trick of Knowledge That Does Not Believe In Beauty

Castigates itself in the language it clings to
Shielding their eyes from this color called bliss

Could what we are be what we are
Could courage be confusion

Could there be no risk but
Subworlds of color

A pianist is bent
Curved into being

Trained to play
The pre-existing notes

But for the hundred-headed harmonies there is no instrument

        Sadly we are invented
        Simultaneously we cannot claim
        Any instrument ours
        What we play to be ours
        It is never here yet

"Soon" he holds up his arms—a candelabra
Soon he chants in Chinese

Soon I will meet nowhere again
No longer need to evade these villains

These copper-stealing thieves
These structures of time

Am I wrong?

    These butterfly binoculars are Death's new brain
    Orange, pink, and ballerina pain
    Strumming shadow
    Ice-floe
    Arch

Fling me away from these vials of age—

    A scroll rolls out of red desert rage
    Tracks in the desert are the writing of the sky

        It is not special
        It is the writing of the sky

Impatience Must Be Unwillingness

To be blind, I begin

Five thousand years to answer each question
"Are you beginning to understand...people are incoherent..."

> I stumble over
> Your driveway
> Your lawn
> I stress
> The Divine Chariot
> Our Fiery Star
> Your little mouth
> A bible in her hand
> A scarf wrapped

" *'My unity shall not be expressed except through thee,'* the child creator
promises. It is the first promise of love—*'on thee shall be based all
calculations and operations of the world.'* "

I miss my soul like I sit down

As if a choice was ever made

The Opening of the Mouth

Blowing away is also blowing through

I hold a charm of salvation that does not guarantee I do

The act of will is what no one asks of you

The only way to see is to continue to see

The whole world is your body and I've given you my medicine

The Palace of Language

I wanted to be silent

Enchiridion

Walk into the woods
Until you walk

Lower
Into the earth

Until you know
How long this raindrop
Speaks the name you hear

Raindrop, now a name
Eternity, anywhere

"Your rebellion is a muscle of air"

I bulwark my heart against an answer
Maze worthy petrified mirror dark horizontal waterfall
Red light I wait at

Return every day
Every day turns

I delay you
I am the world

I do not say the world
I am a blue bird
around
deep brown
her eyes
watery
She speaks,

"I only want to be an opus
Is there only one moment

I know alone into the sky
We hail our voices into the air"

        Watch
        Each turn of your tongue
        Or lose
        Your words in your brain

        Walk
        Under words
        Under rain
        No place safe from these
        Sounds
                A bird child flies above the city

Flower forever fever
What day is it—*Wednesday*

Loss of hours
Loss of words

      Unalone
      Uncalibrated
           Eros

                The library is lovely
                because old
                grating
                shaky
                only
                the given

light outside pale
falling inwards
a light bulb
the little
joined balls of a
brass string—pulled
A little light only
where I stand
Bibles
old
heavy red black
falling apart
fuming with must
heavy with voice
must
I choose
arch my hip up
to the shelf
lean a corner
of the book
into my bone
curves, jagged dips
quick plateaus
sudden dots
crescents
of the desert
a record
of lines
the wind has left
hotness
of the sand
each grain a sky
I let my eyes
fall upon the

curve
the vowel
lowers
the lip
chin curving
into lip
catching breath
moving
from the mouth
out
a word is
this step
each of us
now
takes
to lose the meaning
he says
into the center
of it
stop
the blue dawn
of dream
his skin was
blue the dawn
was pink
the world is never
what she—
never a face
caught between
our eyes
the mirror on the wall
an eye

"Who is the hero of Paradise?"

The Eyes Of Others Are What I Remember

Teary eyes that have no help, eyes between embrace and "what would you show me?" Eyes that cannot talk, eyes where words live in the mouth as citrine and between each tear, a word is. Eyes that have no relation. You could call them, in the eyes of an old man, the eyes of a child, yet in the eyes of a child, you see what you saw in the old man, and it is not child-like, for in the child's eyes, there is someone else their eyes are like—some other place implied by the presence of eyes.

What are eyes?

Confused globes of light, open worlds with no end, eyes, maidens to the light—slow, sudden, foreboding, accepting, straining.

A rainbow is suggestive, so is a gray day. Icons of sight perturb interpretation. An orange cone allows ivy to overcome it. A sexy waxy green leaf—sways. The wind cannot be seen, yet the leaves betray its presence. Is wind like feeling, enemy of sight to what eludes sight? Today warm and wafting, causing what I see to move.

Marionette the leaves are of this warmth, obscene because unseen, hidden like a deep secret is revealed by being kept—all the leaves tell.

A Tantric Measure

Don't you think greed, like other told sins, are made up just to make life dramatic? That even sins are invented, so the void of life that paws for reason, pines for drama, a stage to make life ricochet, walls to kindle what has no appetite for dimension?

And in the post office, while waiting—saw a board covered with the business cards of people. So this is what people do to survive—they categorize themselves. They make their very selves into products, into a service summed up in a sentence.

Endless selves become little language, written on pocketable rectangles—cards, pinned onto a board in a post office. A part of me thought—these people are trying to be of service, aiming to give something. Polis, people—a pole or a steeple—what public structure are their eyes hearkening to in order to see?

What I see is The Tree of Life collapsed onto a single plane—a one-dimensional square. A board. Bored. One person was a psychotherapist—another woman was of a group of women gardeners, called, "Wonder Women Gardeners." Another man fixed instruments on Martin Luther King Way.

This is not the Tree of Life but a board of scattered souls, pinned, as if by the neck—a collection of contractions, each petitioning for a name, an outer planetary body to compel them out of their earthen coordinates. This board houses coordinates craving constellation. Consolation in constellation. A constellation is a relation of coordinates speaking of the space between. This makes sadness bright. This makes singleness—signless.

I saw each card as only I. I thought of *I and Thou*, saw Martin Buber's face ¾ turned toward the reader. Yosefa spoke of God punishing the

Assyrians for conquering and punishing the inhabitants whose land they took to be their own. She added, "but notice how God is acting just like the Assyrians—he is punishing and conquering them for their punishing and conquering."

How I hear this now is language bound. A bounty of words bound by words. In Hebrew, the root for "anger" is also the root for "Hebrew" as well as the verb "to pass". The story of Israel, the origin of Hebrew, I hear now, turn the narrative, prod the plot—the story of the soul of a place, of a language that has not yet learned how to love itself.

Shibboleth. The word you speak to stay alive, the card you give to cross the river, in the sounds you think asked of you, and if lucky break through to The Tree of Life where there is no river you have to cross by sounds made to dam the body of water before you get there. Where the sound you are, the card you give, or fail to give, is what you see. Pieces of wood constructed like stacked children's blocks, each side coming to a point, an arched trellis-like triangle I walk through.

I began to think of objects that are worshipped. I thought of them as warships, not out at sea, but on land, or like the Capricorn is a sea-goat, not land goat, the sign of an animal grounded, not in what is here, but has its hooves in the water that is our unconscious. I saw objects of worship as ships combatting our continuously malleable minds springing from wells of inner earth, resting in each graven image—instructions, goading the mind to images of beings, urging, *See, See*.

I saw around the pictures of great beings, from Mother Mary, down to the level of celebrity, dismal, half-conscious celebrations of the physical forces of attraction, magnetisms, gravity, thangkas where thought is taught in the center of the image that is the form of the teacher. Surrounding the teacher are figures partially seen, almost-other images, connected, yet peripheral, but each still of this created world for our eyes to practice beauty, to jettison happening.

The stress of light is the bark of shadow. I lean towards nuance, empty the chiaroscuro of impermanence into the root of the word. Buddhist cosmology redresses, fixes, the unity of male and female energies by re-coursing the organization to be male—lunar, female—solar.

Qualities of planetary influence and containment in relation to gender evidence in essence to be momentary relations, not fixed connections between man and woman, but energies.

Not only bodies, but similar to how planets orbit, these energies course through the bodies of individuals, of man and woman, each translations of the male and female energies.

And male and female energies are too translations, of an invented need to speak, erecting a hermeneutic however idiosyncratic or heuristic, sounds sounded to séance a somewhere so speaking can serve us.

We will do what we can to continue our leading illusions of speech and need, even if that means assigning the star to the woman and the moon to the man.

I Am A Drama Not Between Man And Woman But Between Time And No Time

The word paradox wedges—a sex full-blooded yet without body.
"It is not the words you say, but how you say them." These hollow
shells, these barnacles. Love affair with pain eyesight is the wizard of.
Allegory of the war between eye and skin.

The young woman with black curly hair projects her soul onto a
Tibetan man. She sucks her soul back in, then projects into the dark,
onto a large white screen. They call this *movie*—for her it is "passage
of soul".

I escort her out of the car, into the theater where her passage is to
be projected impersonally into the eyes, awash onto the faces of the
eager crowd. She whispered to me earlier, "It took me a long time to
realize love is blind."

Later our paths meet by a door. Her eyes are clearly open. No part
of her is looking, yet her gaze is not vacant. Her eyes are teary, not
sorrowful—snow. The sentence she says flows out from her. Her
sentence is what she sheds.

Only now has her sentence returned with a question. Is love blind like
wind, blowing through the world, irrelevant to what it picks up, to
what it blows over? Does love have a mind, and all we can be, shore
to a wave, arms that are open?

"It is not that I like what you write—I like how much you write,"
broken bottles smoothed into glass, testaments and souvenirs from
what goes and comes.

A fat white woman has forgot what is open. The man I met who
was an owl almost cried. This music is making my feelings change.

Parallel autonomies frustrate the unconditioned. Next to a chain link fence, in pitch black glasses, she sucks in the smoke of a long white ocean.

What Do You Do When You Are The Whole World?

When each image cracks open like a poorly built pot? When no image, no identity remains.

When the confusion of the human race is a spectacle of evasion, grabbing for names, for masks—even, simply, clothing, anything to hide this nakedness, this voluptuous truth…

Are all relationships hallowings?

Kindlings of the first fire of meeting. Shells made with the ornaments of days, protecting the first moments when your eyes were ocean and there was no life between us, no fears of leaving, no fears of who else is there—only the thrill of body and time, of the soul that falls in the place of a rhythm, your body that is dawn and my eyes spectacles of one star after another falling asleep in the arms of their mother star our sun who hides her children in her heart that is the day?

Are you aware of your image?

I see you in splices—a soul steeped in matter cannot separate—the plague of immediacy skirting psychosis, over-embellished images, prognosis of the plague—what plague, only an empty place, a failure or a fear or a whisper—a caress to obey the gate, unlock crisis and behave life's chance.

You turn around. Your wife has not been turned to salt. Eurydice has not fallen back into the realm of shades. Each wife, meaning each image, has fallen into your heart that is your gaze—the fire hydrant and the bench you think to sit on, no longer fixtures of the atmosphere, but angles of what you are—all you are now being where you are.

How does your mind survive such saturation?

Deep invisibility and yet you have a body—afternoon light flown by
the ocean through the century beleaguered bumped glass windows
subduing outside escapading edges of the docked boats into an
inside light faintly suggesting things outside, and the names of those
things, by a heat unknown to things, begins to know, falls, onto the
old printing machine, onto the splintering gray hairs of your teacher,
shining around her kind countenance, bristles of an evergreen tree,
how the young woman whose black slipper shoes fit her feet perfectly,
her long legs equally into her dark jeans, and she speaks so casually,
seems to be so proud of her drag-queen friend named Sonny who
she is going to see perform tonight, how she tells this to the boy she
works with, how his breath leaps when he asks her, "Is Robin going
to meet you there?" and you feel his whole heart cradled towards
her, desiring her in her perfectness, in her short silken hair, cut at
a fashionable edge, causing it to coyly curl around the nape of her
neck, how she treats his heavy open heart as a tiny pin—

Where Is Another Taste, Another Scent, Another Place, Where I May Be Reminded Of Change?

The scientific is haunted by another image, a cardiovascular masterpiece of color that in its depth overturns autumn, cannot calculate the seasons so shows in the dark, conceals in the dark, a pale light smuggling prediction.

Inside such contraband, I put my hands. Is this a place where I may remain? Is this a place where I will be so absorbed, so loved into the sun, that all thought of other place will disappear into my skin I will look at when I think to know, when I think to play knowing, when the traffic light remained red but in my gut I thought green, so went forward, breaking a law of color?

Is place only place when you wish to be some other place? Does place mean speech, mean, you can only speak the atmosphere you are in—limitations of the resonance of the angel, counterpoints of cactus, of iron bars guarding nurseries, angels are prey to as we are?

Are angels of the disappearance that creates the arch, the being who curves as the sun appears to curve? Highlight of illusion descending—the lower angels being only a little more so unrestrained by distance.

A voice is holy for a voice is never place—fetishizing matter as our minds crave the physical, losing the audacity of loss—of loss, the shipwreck a household chair is, no one to marry her. There she sits, lonely mahogany, succumbing to the tired body of her absent mate.

An image becomes what you enter and not what you create, or is entering an image a form of creating that image? Is sitting in a city a form of dying? Is tourism a despondency of creation? Is looking at a thing a loss of vision into what a voice suggested you see?

The romance of each place is displaced. Another rhythm invades melody.

I try to strike like the sun strikes but there is a statue of Giordano Bruno who was quiet and made his peace his mind, was burned at the stake. Surrounding him now is a piazza where trashy cheetah like men and women devour pizza and beer. Around his bronze, robe-covered body, bowing with his hands in prayer, Bruno's ghost mutters,

> "Finally, this is place, when I am not here. No place knows voice, can hold a heart—for I, anomaly, I, woe of words, anachronistic sundering, what place can't take, disregard of theme, negligence of order for a crate of silk.
>
> Let me follow you on the path that is far from me. Let me hear so as to know who you are not. Voice, a tunnel I gladly take—the underground railroad I saw as a real train people took underneath America to escape America.
>
> Beasts of burden execute beauty.
>
> We pray for place to find the place inside of place, that sheds place, throws off diatribes of any devotion, who in every scent of beauty, goes alone."

"How come we're talking about this with a language that isn't this? We're talking about the fact that the language has to be different. We're talking about it in the language that isn't different. How can we possibly be there? You may think it's all your problem. Dirac, in the *Scientific American*—this is the thing that just really haunts me—comes to a place where he says, 'Since we know that we have no answers, we must have the wrong questions, and that means we have the wrong language.' And he's talking about Physics."

Robert Duncan, *A Meeting of Poets &
Theologians to Discuss Parable, Myth &
Language,* 1968

La Rimulate

accustomed
ocean
to speaking
      trincolalas
accustomed
      messo
to writing
      mi madorney
in the forms
      sincopate
the costumes
we call

Language—we body
hyla
    our innocence
vac
    dim
      the bliss of

                        ahava
        the immortalling
                        umishpatim
        instrument
                                        balilah   undula

Only her feeling there, the tone of her
A purple tone waves out from her
A man picks up a shiny chain

Weightlessness of words
As if talking was
As if the vortex of

Tessitura
We tone it down
So it happens over time
So it is what we call time

What we have done to what does not happen
We could call Language

Dissolution Ventriloquiet

Rose silent boxes of my breath boulevard begonia
Fire escapes fire twinkle blue handicap botanical snake ever eve said
Sentence, sentience

Lilith little girl big bang land locked sunsets sing things logic jewelry
The eyes, her earring
Hearing opalized
Send her to the evergreen leaves let the sun fall
Dowse her

Hypnotized heaven heaver unweaving white
Rapture Chinese written script words ornaments weld a child
Frightened amiable liquid amber voice just the sun again
Sleep hidden bright

Mountain
Hot

Mother
Water

Saying
Bellying

Wildflower
Free her

Sunflower
A man is

Free her
No tools

Haven shadows make smoke logos men hunt ivy swaying ivy
Glass scorn cup

Samadhi equal memory
Swim a sure shore

Magenta wait
Himma water

Silly girl a Wednesday morning daughter dark breath choice grows
Becomes the world

Psyche swimming places to sleep
She eyebrows earth a person turning in the wind

Human hum
Be rational
Ra   tion
Your   in   tu   ition
Ition   nation
Ition   tu
Ition   in
Ition
Ra
          under lullabies

African shadows nomenclatured mandala copper plumbing plow her
Kiss awakens, continues

Shangri la vernacular
The letters roots freeing her
The letters keys the life and so he said

SAY IT

Spell
OPEN

Stuff and much and yet and for and could have been purpura
Golden sinus linear strangling angles of radial heart to be all and
Breathing

Are you speaking something speaking?

Small world angst of a mantle in summer
Feather learned meridian

The number eight autonomous
Into earth the name

In a man's mouth
At the end of a day

Coarse smile
And begin in time

Snow Maiden Shimmering Suffering

Of the tiniest filaments of language
The heart too is inventing heat

"Don't make anything"
Suddenly I could hear

Could "coil and recoil with the lash"
Eyelash, basic pain of looking

Raw diffidence of knowing
Mesosphere, distrusting knowing

A falling lash, a thin invasion
We hide and call our hiding, knowing
Permitted by the artifice of knowing

When the marine thick with seaweed rises out of the water
Camouflaged by bioluminescent reconnaissance

Our fields of human knowledge
Are also shields
Can be shields

Knowledge, a shroud
Can be a cool cloth
After the volcano
A memorial washing away the contortions of a face

To go on living—hide
Inside repeated acts insured by the authority of the name called
Knowing
But then, again—this is Language

I am riding
The edge of the letter O
On the heel of a name

This red knowledge
This worldless devotion
This necessity—

"The more you are caught, the more you are free"

Too much talking
Too much freewheeling

Each one must somehow deliver into the animal of another
The overwhelming ecstasy of sun

PULSIONS—
Arc any language not knowing language
Not knowing its Eternity is itself

Arc this language into muscle
Into blood
Into dread
An eyelash is a fever—twilight

Honed   Desert   Venus

Oil   alone   quivering

Windmill, remember

Hell: when language thinks it knows

Hell is everywhere

Bear Me

Mountain Artemisia cut
Sky arrow
Bow mind back

Hunt canker hawk cry
Crescent sheep born

Moon oven bear
Edge of wood
Snow
Wolf

She wolf
She city born he

Womb becomes answering
Hollow candida

Root can't
A name city snow

Carbon brother
Nevada blood sierra
Moon truce

Human tone
Knowledge dodecahedron
Born wood

Leaf breath lead
Mouth husk horizon
Amazon'd mind

Jaw German
Score of music scar

Listening leaf of the oak brain street
Obeying branches princes princess
The Great Tree

Oddness Of Difference

Mute of spirit
Alive, recall

"Follow your...

       Bliss follows nothing—
       A moment, an oak
       Apology

       A line of light burning tenderness no other tongue

       Syllable wind of mirror
       Worlds wheel into wild ground

       My plate: iron, spoken, faint

       Prism
       I might be wrong but I am rain
       It rained

       A light bulb in a vase

       End I say sphere
       A rosary of sun

       A rhythm in the warning of a raspberry

Entering A Poem Is Entering A Garden

Eyeing a bench agreeing
I will go there, sit down, take rest

Say, dear mind

Sleep in words a dreaming where
Waking is no different than

A slumber here

Where will you fall
Let me cradle you

Do you not understand
What the world does in you

What was that—the way his lip quivers
He wakes from sleep into a word

A poet now
For words are what he learns
To waken into

Eyes, Do You Not See

Swept to the edges, gestures cascade
Huddle question, mother object

As our eyes let
Light rain lets

The light around the day is
Let only our eyes
Of having seen

Light, we could be lost
Welcome in entrance

Held from the world shed
Without menace

Eyes, do you not say

Leave me in my suddenness
Know me only suddenly

Let me be without you
So you may be with me

Wind Blows There Is No One To Hold Except Hold Me

Artifice prolifically helpless
King of little things counting all the things

Out of the sand dunes, asks,

> "Have you ever learned an instrument?
> The vision was a trick."

Rock, the language a fulfillment of all others
In her absence, The Tower of Babel

> A rabbit hops out of a tiger's urn

> Is love a white vase tigers envy?
> Is the only way to love you to be all of you?

Hold me hummingbird
Fly me to your castle of nervous love

> Do you watch wind?

> Realities huddle
> Overhead a helicopter flies

> The wind's eye we gather
> Together under

> To say the word soul is not a word

The Rose She Serves

Taste equal to scent
A single Chinese letter
Is a temple

Many letters
Running down the page
Are many temples

You have only to open your mouth
A temple is you
Opening your mouth

Her eyes open wide
"Finally," she says

"You may eat everything"

Paramitayana A Woman Walks Towards Me

"From the perspective of Neoplatonic piety the notion that 'the one' would be compelled by anything, even its own nature, is viewed with horror."

Faith is a face snake-skinning listening

Protected by what I cannot prove
I have no mind but Antenna Louisiana

Modern buildings white walls give us
Horseback shining in the glare of one thousand mirrors

No one knows me, desire of a rainbow
Speaking from ocean cave to ocean cave

A sigh gives birth to an island without need

Sometimes we just
Say what we hear

When I say I want to be alone I only mean a voice which is alone
Could be with everyone I love

A necklace we grip between our teeth, pretend to be our speech

To be said is to be given a mirror
By looking into a mirror you see what you are and then walk on

She Said Why I Saw It As A Feather

An obelisk behind
A sigil one hides
One's smallness behind

Elaborate
Seductive letter
Serpent letter

Let us little elves hide

She Tries To Study

One by one
The contours of
One letter

What am I asking for when I say I seek the origins of language?

If she lets her eyes rest upon the finest edge
       Willowing in which destination is deserving of not sought
Maybe then she will learn how to think
       Do I want to know how language was first used?
Maybe then no thought
       There was only one we walked up to it
Will arch
       We watched as each one held it
Or undermine
       A shadow
Her
       In her mouth until she died

       Or am I asking to enter what is not restricted by evidence?

Kabbalah The Traffic Light

Each word a chariot
Pulled by horses
White lights glow down the sides

A man holds the reins
Two people
Sit in the back

Suddenly
No chariot, no horses

Only a man
Two tourists walk behind

All in a daze
No one knowing the other

I Step Into The Only Room I Know

Air, an edge, hide
Stripped from animal

Triangular blade carving sun into shadow

"FUGGE L'OMBRA COL
SOL COL SOL' RITORNA
MA L'UOM QUAL OMRA
FUGGA E PIUNONTORNA"

Fontana Giuseppe, 1855

"The shade goes away with the sun
With the sun, it returns
But the man from this shade
Goes away
And does not return."

I Have A Boat No One Rides In

I don't know where it is
But I pray to it

The wood of the boat lips
Across cold cave water

I hear voices I call my own
Voices I claim
To be the ones I've heard

Voice—the word alone
Containment of sound by someone
Bizarre in a world of infinite utterance

Each voice I hear I long not to hear
The wood beneath me—soft, splinters

Egyptian false door
False star outside the mind true only for its beckoning

Reign of the eye
Reign of the ear

Sekhmet was a defender of the creative order, not a creator of it
Did you ever think, have you ever thought, it is better to be here?

Stacks of books, miracles, air and water, the cover, the weather

You present a new imagining where all the whimsy in me of other
Times, other worlds, other Egypts, other eyes

All the swell of what else could be or was

Becomes an unexplained shine
I cannot believe I am granted to feel

My imagination becomes your eyes
Looking with me
Into your eyes

        Isolation of entrances
        My head is in my hands

        I learn to feign that which I am
        Circumambulation, prostration

I learn to change the movements I have come to call myself in

But the bright light
The naked body I call my own
As if the body I answer—

        This too is an illusion of this place
        Out of which voices
        Thrash

        Fly about in their many
        Direction'd flight

        Chorus chaos—
                All flock, all fly away

What Will You Hold Real Against Your Death?

Will it be some ancient esoteric text?

Or will it be a person most close to you
You hold with every last breath in you

Against what takes you from your breath

Subhadrapurusha: to swell, to burn, to complete
An act of breathing
And the only place to ever speak

A place that burns with the roots you choose
And finds itself in the skin of a word

Roots so ready they
Unknowingly intertwine

Long enough to make the roots a word
Long enough to make the word a god

Or did the god come first
Did she rain or dance or cry
Down upon the ground

Forcing herself back into a word
Down into the roots

Our final memory of her
Our last sense of intellect

Before she
A power from which

We seek a depth of speech
Why the roots of words are called
Roots

Before they were gods
They were ground

Letter Is A Number

Does not count
Barely sees

Wraps itself around itself
I.

Wet flesh
Me.

Sweltering in his lack of breath
He longs for women's breasts like he longs to feel the ends of his own
Brain

Pour myself into myself
Cistern what I will never be of what I will never be

I am nothing but curiosity
A fabulous grid, gaudy, in flames, trying to find underneath my
Dress—

You can only make a body of time if you relate the pre-believable
Vocabularies of flesh

She sought to be minute
Hate could never be the end

Running in circles
To make a mound of
Earth, wheels to be heard

This life within her—a strawberry needing to be soaked
This blue gut

She had always been an end

In the end
There is an inside

Lady Screams Out In Moonlight

CUT the surfaces of words
Words are not slippery sounds here
Words are not coy implications

Words are rings
She stretches her legs across a gorge
Cries out for a bridge to lay her body down

Are you tracing the labyrinthine toils of tongues?
Are you hollowing linearity out a heart caressed in the found?
Is this time I bite myself into?

My joy of bodying what I name overheats
I turn my words, I find the way
I enter here is carved

This is no knowledge
This poetry
Is no knowledge

Or it is to its utmost
Surrounded by a moat of fear

In the pit of ignorance stands Minerva
Well dressed yet nervous

She has no thought in her
Yet everyone came here
To worship her

Vowels And Consonants Block The Way

Enter by vowels and consonants

"The busy chores of thought and action fail to stem the surge of yearning from my heart."

7th Dalai Lama (1708–1757)

Know window No window
Say window Say sand

One word is saving another
From rest, itself
Sand—Open

A rain curl sun is
Gold ripples thoughts are treasure I hold up to the

Sun a stone is
A shadow nothing thinks

In Vain, Manzanita

In my veins
Black dome endangered
Light, goodbye

"Some people fear the imagination"

He swings in circles
A disc, red laser
Geometric figures

Voice minsk manzanita

Trusted statues before—they spoke, were from their cages, birds
Released

"The intellectual love of a thing consists in the understanding of its
perfections. All creatures whatsoever desire this love."

She kept on sending ribbons into the wind
Tossing ribbons over her balcony
Into the ocean

Bird just in reach of the olive branch it flies in front of

Procession of the guides
Vesuvius nuns
Pullulation

The longest vessel is the shortest sound
The need for abstract language

The Northern Lights held across time

How to stay awake in the far away land

When you speak with all worlds you are only speaking
Vengeance all forms now

A fantastic system suddenly remembers
The dance around the golden calf

All creation myths
Look themselves in the eye

In the shock of Narcissus
Children are patches of gas
No one has sense strong enough to name

A color is a minute
In the age of light
Men are what they see

They cannot plan
But they can enter
Their own eyes

Each kid holds a piece of the snake
The Merry Artifact
The Anthropomorphic Teller

"The pursuit of knowledge did not have to be in spite of the
Happiness of angels"

Everywhere I go the king is naked

Reminding the wiring alone
Her offering is an open tone

What was yearned for here is what sings and is heard
City that makes you see

She seems to feel sorry for the fact she has senses
There was no rain because they prayed for rain

Nothing in the world will support your deepest task

A man with swollen hands asks you what the world is
A new vice of puppeteering will haunt your power

"The control (*taṣarruf*) of things, the power to work miracles, is a
secondary aspect; the greatest mystics refrained from exerting this
power, often with contempt, partly because they knew that in this
world, the servant cannot become the Lord, and that the subject who
dominates a thing (*mutaṣarrif*) and the thing he dominates (*mutaṣarraf
fīhi*) are essentially one being, but also because they recognized that
the form of what is epiphanized (*mutajallī*) is also the form of what
the epiphany is revealed (*mutajallà-lahu*)."

Henry Corbin, *The Heart as a
Subtile Organ*

The Silent Voice, Revealed

In its reticence
The wonder of who we never were nor are

Your birthday on a cross I honor
You say—No, I ask voice from you

I walk up to the body I walk up to
She leans her face inside a widely open road

He drives her up the hill says
Heart not fear

They collect seeds from strange worlds to suck

Voice grows into trees
They lie back releasing life

Leave in the imprints of their elbows, resonance
A pleasure of gravity collapsing into memory

As the evening is a star
Hurry forth into a touch

A twisting into
Are you

Her name, a hat worn
In the desert

To hide under
To count time under

She walks up to a star
Her voice strains toward

"When the artist [alchemist] sees the perfect whiteness, the
philosophers say that one has to destroy the books because they have
become superfluous." Pernety, 1758

The sun is the most constant traveler
In our wandering solar system

But a white heat learns to speak
Imagination's beast and lord golden in a bowl

Language now a home, if not—then?
Overaccumulated matter of vivid moments untouched by intelligence

Find a mirror not in form
The sign is the mind that sees

Relaxing into metonymies, The Mind, The Magic Lantern

Precession of the Perihelion
Our eyes wands waving pendulums premeditating the awakening

And then after my plunge into flesh, I was suspended in the ends of
My effort
The end of my flesh

Or a chance to change my fate
By the fossils letters face

                      Irrefutability swallows days dispassionately
                      Thoughts pass exclaiming the desire to be
                      What they have no intention of being

The women who walk backwards
The being neither god, demigod, nor hell geing, but one who moves
Through all

Swan across
                                        Night Depository

I punch through copper busts of men of knowledge
In the silent reading room
I pity boys and girls who have not felt through
The weight of books

How do I know now?

I go in the night alone
Under the moon I walk
Through a wood of wild pigs

I am scared
But if I make
Each step
Without worry
I am safe

                    He realizes he is not the world so he
                    Becomes the world

                    The sun ribs in gold
                    Meadow of the old

                    A song no one denies

Coloratura

Nuns sit around sipping lemonade in Pompeii waiting to see the
Painting of Mary the only remain long after Vesuvius
Cerulean

Nothing is wrong except this road

The Hollow Earth
A silhouette engraving

Bisbigliando
What is a line, accomplished by air

Naming upon naming
Under, into, naming

I like you like every other afternoon in an alien sun
Amber, ardent

Are nomads sad
Who is anyone looking for anything

Saltshakers made of stainless steel
Sentiment, Sediment

Guard it with your life—

Could I move my life so as to guard
The most precious element of Earth

       No place

             The birds flew up from the brick path, up the
             Sides of the building, around, through the
             Trees, away

Upholding the orange against the lifelessness of the sphere

"The awake must be awake"

Purgatory is the distance between your hand
Agog, cherishing a spoon

Days are evangelical

Eyes moving is a human
Chin in hand
Index finger pointing upward

The wind gives me a habit
Hierarchies of soul

"Wherever we are, we are creatures of other places. Whenever
we are, creatures of other times. Whatever our experience, we are
creatures of other imagined experiences. Not only the experience of
unity, but the experience of separation, is the mother of man. The
very feeling of melody at all depends upon our articulation of the
separate parts involved."

What do you mean continue
What do you mean go on

A river is continue
Your face is voice

He hears her words as he drives the car forward through a field of
Flowers, apples on the sides of the road

Only his eyes see
Everyone around him

The radiance of the clock
The shining of the measure of his mind

The solidity of time
The passing of a soul

Voice skitters toward voice alone

Your birthday on the cross
Reds white

All your thinking not to be honored
All my honor of you, not honored

But to be laid
Lined

On grooves of
Madam Earth

Compromise instruction
Valiant pangs

A Note On The Text

Quoted material is sometimes attributed, sometimes partially attributed, to its author, text, or time. *Archipelago* is not methodical, nor in a broader sense scholarly, but is searching for a dissolution of mind in music where each utterance bears a vector of its movement. At the instance of each quote, I chose whether to mention the author, text, or time, depending on how the presence or absence of such information sounded in the surrounding field. I am not trying to pinpoint sources, neither am I intent on obscuring them, but am interested in how context disrupts or deepens a lyrical absorption.

Acknowledgments

Thank you Mikki, my mother, for raising me in gentleness, for showing me how to care and feel the peace of the world. Thank you Michael, my father, for exposing me to literature and the mirthful play of words. Thank you Aviva, my sister, for joining me in my imagined worlds. Thank you Aunt Susie for providing me with a haven in New York City, and showing me the power and potential of a single woman's soul, and to my grandparents, Ruth and Edgar Bondy, for your warmth and heavenly guidance, and to all of my extended family, the Bondys and the Siegels, for being with me from my youngest years until now, unconditionally welcoming and loving.

Thank you George Quasha and Susan Quasha for grounding me in my life as a poet, surrounding me with kindred creations of artists past and present, and for your great compassion and generosity of mind and heart towards the publication of this book, and so many books of others. Additionally, thank you, Susan, for devoting so much of your time to the cover design, for infusing the book with your beauty and skill. Thank you Sam Truitt for being a presence of consistent encouragement, patiently and gallantly chaperoning *Archipelago* into form.

Thank you Robert Kelly, to whom this book is dedicated, for giving me my life in writing, the contentedness of content, a continuous attention, ever interested, intimate, naturally offering. Thank you Charles Stein for guiding me to the edge of the mind's language, and showing me how there is still language there, and what it sounds like, and for talking with me seemingly forever about everything it's possible to talk about. Thank you Peter Lamborn Wilson for versing me in the crossroads of politics and poetry, for the spirit of re-search, of how to recover lost stories, people, plots of land, how to go to sites of psychic deprivation and witch them into possibilities of living. Thank you Alia Johnson for your vastness, your frankness, and for offering me a place to begin *Archipelago*, in the gentle woods of Barrytown, to contemplate a church of crystals and sculptures from which I became acquainted with the secret life of things. Thank you Lissa Wolsak, Queen of Poetry Across the Border, elegant diaognal, for your ruthless uniqueness amidst a world of generalities. Thank you Steven D. Goodman, performance artist of sixteen kinds of nothingness, for leading me to invaluable moments of mind through the brightness of language. Thank you Diane di Prima for your bold incarnation, for living in the authority of soul and the holiness of poetry. Thank you Juliana Spahr for being such a powerful force in the Bay Area, for helping so many young writers find their ground, and for generously agreeing to read my manuscript and comment upon it.

Thank you Elizabeth Snowden for flying with me through The Gateway of the East into the flowers of Berkeley, and for being my twin sister of impossible speech. Thank you Nico Peck, clear-seeing soul of commanding view, for being my guide and friend in our City of Celestial Musicians. Thank you David Brazil for tearing open the outside world, displaying how I could through every language possible live a life of soul alongside the souls of others. Thank you Sara Larsen for bearing a Sapphic ray of crystalline, revolutionary kindness, for loving the intelligence of the body and its politic.

Thank you Andrew Kenower for inviting me down from the hills into the streets of Oakland, into the households of poets and the happiness of companionship. Thank you Laura Woltag for being an elemental ally yearning for a deeper outside. Thank you Zach Houston for being my friend outside of time, transcending each transaction with the fast trust of mystic kinship. Thank you Yosefa Raz for questioning origins, for confronting history with poetry and poetry with history. Thank you Amy Berkowitz for your steady, canny, ear and heart. Thank you Lara Durback for dancing the strength of the printed word and the embossed vocation of activist and poet, and for your gentleness. Thank you Brandon Brown for adventuring thought ancient and modern, jovially, openly and with indefatigable curiosity and humanity. Thank you Alli Warren for being a dwelling of poetic depth and insight, ever honed. Thank you Lindsey Boldt for divining reverie, and empathy, and mobile ingenuity. Thank you Steve Orth for gleaning hilarity, and bouyancy and thoughtfulness. Thank you Ted Rees for your wildness and exactness within every wilderness.

Thank you to every poet I have read, heard, or met, for the depth of your vow, and the power of your creations. If I have left your name out, know that *you* are not left out. I wanted to thank everyone I have known, and maybe in some way that's the work of poetry and will be the task of another book.

Afterword

She kept on thinking she was wrong. Then, she thought she was right. Then the rug said, "I am the nature of the universe." The wicker stool said, "I am the nature of the universe." The white orchid said, "I am the nature of the universe." They all laughed together, as laughter was the nature of the universe too—but in buckets of being casting an underbelly for each one to embark into a light of uprightness; they would tomorrow sleep inside the witness of their names.

But what if tomorrow is a name too and tomorrow sleeps as we do? Is it still possible to meet inside a place that is asleep?

Yes, lulled tomorrow, even more so than the day. The door knob that is a cobra, the paper blowing on the sidewalk that is a dragon, the boy's squinting eyes that are the words he can't see in you, the dark woman who drives a great boat through small streets, the girls laughing, punching digits with their pinkies, the old man who comes with bags full of little books and gives one to everyone except you, and then he gives you one, a different one, a nomad eyelash one that only blinks when it has reached its place of pilgrimage—the nerves inside your body that are strings on her father's old guitar, scarred—she smiles—and beautiful, she walks down the stairs, and then she says her name.

Alana Siegel was born in Los Angeles in 1985. She graduated from Bard College in 2007, earning a B.A. in Language and Literature. *Archipelago* is her first full-length book of poetry. Her chapbooks include *The Occupations*, *Semata*, and *words from Ra Ra Junction*. She presently lives in Berkeley, California, collaborating at the burgeoning Bay Area Public School.

CPSIA information can be obtained at www.ICGtesting.com
Printed in the USA
BVOW01s0453080914

365120BV00008B/74/P